Best wishes to Yvette

from Monsieur Poulet. See you soon Mr Chicken

PHOTOGRAPH OF BEARER

SIGNATURE OF BEARER
MR CHICKEN

PASSPORT
NAME
MR CHICKEN
PLACE AND DATE OF BIRTH
UNKNOWN.
HEIGHT
4 Metres +
COLOUR OF HAIR
EVERYTHING YELLOW

Looking forward to seeing you, Monsieur Poulet!
Yvette

Words I may need to know in Paris

English		French
hello	–	bonjour
goodbye	–	au revoir
arrivals	–	arrivées
departures	–	départs
madam	–	madame
mr	–	monsieur
mr Chicken	–	Monsieur Poulet
superb	–	superbe
thank you	–	merci
tickets	–	billets
tourist bus	–	bus de touristes
yes	–	oui
magnificent	–	magnifique

This book belongs to...

Places I must see...!?

Eiffel Tower - called Tour Eiffel.

Louvre Museum - is called Musée du Louvre

Palace of Versailles - is called Château de Versailles

Notre Dame - is called Notre Dame de Paris Cathédrale

Mr Chicken goes to Paris

(Monsieur Poulet va à Paris)

Leigh HOBBS

BLOOMSBURY

LONDON BERLIN NEW YORK SYDNEY

For Julia Murray

Bloomsbury Publishing, London, Berlin, New York and Sydney

First published in Great Britain in September 2010 by Bloomsbury Publishing Plc
50 Bedford Square, London, WC1B 3DP

First published by Allen & Unwin Pty Ltd, Sydney, Australia

Mr Chicken Goes to Paris copyright © Leigh Hobbs 2009
The moral right of the author/illustrator has been asserted

A CIP catalogue record of this book is available from the British Library

ISBN 978 1 4088 0524 4

5 7 9 10 8 6 4

Printed in China by Toppan Leefung Printing Ltd, Dongguan, Guangdong

Cover design by Leigh Hobbs & Sandra Nobes
Text design by Sandra Nobes

All papers used by Bloomsbury Publishing are natural, recyclable products
made from wood grown in well-managed forests. The manufacturing
processes conform to the environmental regulations of the country of origin

Thanks to Sandra Nobes, Sheralyn Bavinton, Ric Benson and Elise Jones for their invaluable assistance
And of course Erica Wagner, without whom this book . . .

www.bloomsbury.com/childrens
www.leighhobbs.com.au

Mr Chicken loved to travel.
His French friend Yvette had invited him to visit,
so he studied his maps, grabbed his camera
and caught a taxi to the airport.

Mr Chicken flew to France.
Paris, to be exact …

... economy.

As the clouds parted, Mr Chicken
was thrilled to see Paris way down below.
'Fasten your seat-belt please, sir,' said the air hostess.
'We are about to land.'

When he arrived, Yvette was there to greet him.
'Bonjour, Monsieur Poulet. Welcome to Paris.'
'Bonjour, Yvette!' said Mr Chicken. 'How wonderful to see you!'

Mr Chicken was tired after his long flight, but rest was out
of the question. He was keen to see the sights, so Yvette
bought a museum pass and travel card for two.

After years of looking at pictures in books,
Mr Chicken could hardly believe he was really in Paris.

On the way to the Arc de Triomphe,
he politely asked someone to take his photo.
'Of course, monsieur,' came the reply.
'Merci, madame,' said Mr Chicken.

On top of the Arc de Triomphe
he studied his list of helpful
French phrases and cried, 'Magnifique!'

Mr Chicken took lots of photos for his
album before he and Yvette hopped
back on the bus. It was time to see some
art at the Musée du Louvre.

After five minutes, Mr Chicken was exhausted.
He was thinking of sitting down and having a cake when
Yvette said, 'Look, the Mona Lisa!'

'It's lovely,' said Mr Chicken, licking his lips.
He took a photo, and bought a postcard.
Best of all, he found a special Mona Lisa tea-towel
for his kitchen back at home.

Soon after, there was a strange
rumbling in Mr Chicken's tummy.
'Er, pardon me,' he said.
'Maybe we should have lunch?'
said Yvette.
'Oh, yes please, er, oui! Oui!' said
Mr Chicken, practising his French.

'Superbe!' he said, after
enjoying two frog-leg soufflés
on board the tourist boat.

To help him blend in
and feel French,
Yvette took Mr Chicken
for a ride on the Métro.

All went well until
he got lost.

To make matters worse,
he forgot his French.
So no one understood
when he asked for help.

What a relief it was when he heard a familiar voice.
'Monsieur Poulet! *This* way to the Eiffel Tower.'
It was Yvette.

The queue was long and Mr Chicken was far too excited to wait for the lift.

So he made his own way to the top, where he and Yvette admired the view.

Back on the streets of Paris, Yvette waited patiently while Mr Chicken had his portrait painted.

He blushed when she said, 'It looks just like you.'

There was so much to do and see and eat in Paris
that Mr Chicken nearly overheated.
Just in time, he found a place to cool down.

'I think we need to go somewhere quiet,' said Yvette.

'This,' Yvette whispered, 'is the most famous church in all of France.'

The inside of Notre Dame was certainly beautiful, but Mr Chicken had his heart set on the roof-top tour.

The roof-top tour was thrilling. What's more, Mr Chicken found a special place to play in the bell tower.

Next was a trip to the Palace of Versailles in a taxi with a sunroof.

'Queen Marie Antoinette lived here,' said Yvette.

Mr Chicken was impressed. In fact, he thought he might like to move in.

'Come,' said Yvette. 'Let's look inside.'

The rooms were huge, and so alas was Mr Chicken's waistline.
'I might have to go on a diet,' he thought in the Hall of Mirrors,
catching a glimpse of a great big bottom.

At dinnertime, however, the diet was forgotten.
'It all looks delicious,' said Mr Chicken.
'I'll have everything on the menu.'

A perfect day was nearly over.

And so was Mr Chicken's visit.
'Au revoir, Monsieur Poulet,' said Yvette, at the airport.
'Au revoir, Yvette,' said a tearful Mr Chicken.

But right at the last minute, there was a great big problem. While his luggage could fit on the plane, poor Mr Chicken could not.

Luckily, clever Yvette came to the rescue with a splendid idea.

So Mr Chicken, and his souvenirs,
could fly home after all ... first class.

What a wonderful day it had been!

Tuesday.

Dear Yvette

Thank you for
a wonderful
day. (merci!)
I shall send
you some
photographs
very soon.
Best wishes from
your friend
monsieur Poulet.

503-03AP

To, Yvette.
Paris
FRANCE.